MISS MAYA
— AND THE —
BRIDGE
TO EVERYWHERE

D1280185

Norman Baron

Cover design and illustrations by 100Covers.com
Book formatting by FormattedBooks.com

eBook ISBN-13: 978-1-7341641-0-7
Paperback ISBN-13: 978-1-7341641-1-4
Library of Congress Control Number:2019916723

DEDICATION

This book is dedicated to *Miss Maya Fisher*, our granddaughter, and the protagonist of the book, ***Miss Maya and the Bridge to Everywhere.*** It is also dedicated to my wife, *Miriam Baron*, without whom none of this would have been possible.

ACKNOWLEDGMENT

My very special gratitude to my excellent mentor, *Marcy Pusey,* who helped me a great deal in my struggle with this book. Her efforts have made it all possible. Marcy went above and beyond to make this dream come true.

Dreams do come true.

Thank you, Marcy.

PROLOGUE

THE ORIGIN OF RANDOLPH

There was an old lady, named Gandola, who had a number of various and sundry critters at her house, mostly cats and dogs. This also included the occasional wolf and lynx cubs, except as they got older, they tried to eat the other animals. Unlike other nutty old hags, she did *not* let them poop in her house until the smell was so bad that the paint peeled from the walls. However, pooping or not, with all of the critters running around the place, the smell was still quite impressive, not to the point of eye-watering, but close to it.

For many years her house was outside of the town, and she was more or less left to her own devices. After a lengthy time, an interstate highway was built north of town. The new and better highways attracted factories and businesses which, in turn, attracted new people and the town grew. It wasn't long before the real estate developers showed up. A house building boom soon followed and the town began to expand—all the way to, and around, the old lady's house.

It isn't hard to imagine that the new neighbors were not happy to live near such a vile smell. Plus, the fact that some of the animals were almost feral and had no respect for property boundaries. Petitions were turned in to the Sanitation Department to have the place condemned and torn down. Needless to say, the old lady was horrified with the prospect of losing her "babies." She was not willing to give up the animals, not even a single one.

The idea was floated that all but one of the animals would be taken away. She would have none of it. A number of the mothers with small children felt sorry for her but there was little that they could do.

One sunny Sunday it came to a head. The dog-pound came with several trucks to take away the dogs.

Gandola screeched and screamed at them and was all set to scratch their eyes out. The dog-pound personnel didn't hesitate to return the favor. The neighbors screamed at the dog-pound people and at Gandola. She also added screaming at the neighbors to her repertoire. It was all going down the old oval drain.

At the height of it all, a small three-year-old girl named Maya came over to Gandola's house carrying a stuffed brown teddy bear. It was almost as big as she was but had only one eye because of a teething accident when Miss Maya was very small. Maya gave her bear to Gandola.

"You won't have all of your animals anymore, but you can have this bear to keep you company and be your friend."

Gandola looked at the very small little girl and thanked her for her generous gift. "But it isn't alive," said Gandola.

"You might be surprised," said the little girl. "What will you name him?"

"The very first dog I ever had was named Randolph," said Gandola. "I will call this little bear Randolph in his honor." After she thanked the little girl again, Gandola smiled to herself as Maya skipped back to her house.

No one knew that she was secretly a powerful witch. She worked her spells as best she could but had to borrow some of the ingredients from her witch friends, at least the few who were still alive. It took several months, but slowly at first, and then with increasing speed, Randolph learned to walk and later on, to talk. Gandola was very happy with Randolph and he with her except, although she took more baths, she still didn't smell very good.

After several months Gandola started to get weak and tired. She no longer walked more than she had to, instead she just shuffled along. Her appetite got worse. She realized that she was dying. She knew that she must give the little bear back to Maya but was too weak to walk over to Maya's house, plus all of Gandola's friends were, by this time, dead.

Gandola crafted a spell that would bring Maya to her house. It took several attempts but finally, with her strength nearly gone, she heard a very soft knocking on her door. She opened it with an opening spell and the little girl came into her house.

"I am going away for a very long time," said Gandola. "I thank you for letting me have Randolph. He has been a good friend to me and in return for your kindness, I would like to give him back to you. I taught him to walk and talk and use his little short arms as best he can. I know that you will be the best of friends. If I return, I will come and see you and Randolph. You need to go home now with Randolph so that your mother doesn't worry. Goodbye Miss Maya and Randolph."

By this time her voice was so soft that even with her sharp little ears Miss Maya had trouble hearing her. A very short time after Maya and Randolph left, Gandola died.

When Maya got back to her house she ran to her mom with Randolph. She told her mom how happy she was to have Randolph back with her and how much she had missed him. Then her smile faded to a sad face and she started to cry.

"What is it?" said Maya's mother.

"Mom, I think that Gandola is dead," said Maya.

"What makes you say such an awful thing, Maya?" said her mom.

"She was so weak, I could hardly hear her talk," said Maya. "Could you and Dad please go over and see her? Maybe we can help her."

Maya's parents hurried next door but came back soon after and called the police. It didn't take much time before the police came, the coroner was called and Gandola's death was confirmed. Maya's parents went around to the neighbors explaining what had happened and asking for donations for her burial. Because of the previous problems with her dogs, and because most of them didn't like her or were just cheap, very little money was raised. Her body remained in her house overnight. Sometime during the night her house burned to the ground. The fire was very hot and intense. When the ashes cooled, no trace of Gandola could be found, not even a single bone.

For a time, everyone speculated endlessly about what might have happened. No answers ever came out of all of the tongue wagging and slowly over time the whole incident faded into the past and was forgotten. There being no heirs, the property was condemned by the city and the debris was cleared away. Even though it was put up for sale by the city, no one bought the property and nothing was ever built there. It eventually grew up to brush, trees, and blackberry bushes. The local children grew up crawling around in the bushes, building forts, and having purple rings around their mouths during blackberry season.

CHAPTER 1

THE COMING OF MARLIN

The old wizard stood on a hill in the desert, staring at the stars. The black midnight surrounded him. In the dark silence he had a vision. There were two little girls, Miss Maya and Bits, plus a small stuffed bear named Randolph who could talk. Something was going to happen soon, something bad.

Miss Maya and Bits were both eleven years old. They had been friends since preschool. The girls both wore jeans, T-shirts, and some badly scuffed tennis shoes. Miss Maya was an elegant little thing which, for some reason, gave her the name that everyone used for her: Miss. It wasn't planned, it just happened that way. Miss Maya wore her light brown hair in a ponytail while Bits wore her dark hair in what looked like an explosion in a hay stack.

Miss Maya held Randolph, her little stuffed bear, who had been her constant companion, confidant, and security blanket as long as she could remember. He had survived her babyhood with only the loss of one eye, the result of Miss Maya's teething phase, which left him with a fear of being eaten. The family was used to seeing her carry her little brown bear as she wandered around the house and played outside. Miss Maya and Randolph were the best of friends despite the teething incident. She included Randolph in just about everything that she did.

"My grandfather built the bridge over the little stream in our garden. I asked him why he built the bridge, and he told me that it was a magical bridge. He called it the Bridge to Everywhere. I think we should go see it," Miss Maya said to Bits.

They soon stood in front of the bridge. Miss Maya leapt around, waving her arms in the air, hardly able to contain her excitement. She paced back and forth, anticipating crossing the Bridge to Everywhere with Bits and Randolph.

"It's time to go," said Miss Maya.

"I don't know," said Bits. "Are you sure it's safe? Are you sure that there isn't something hiding under the bridge that will jump out and gobble us up? If we cross the bridge, can we get back here? I'm getting scared. Maybe we shouldn't go. I think it is probably too dangerous."

"Hmmmm," said Miss Maya with a thoughtful expression. "I think that it's safe, but you could be right, who knows what we will find on the other side, but that is part of the reason that we should go. It's part of the adventure. Maybe we should ask Randolph what he thinks. He is pretty smart you know."

"What does that stupid one-eyed bear know anyway?" said Bits.

"I know a lot more than you think I do, Bits," said Randolph. "After Miss Maya went to bed I used to hear her parents talking with Grandpa and I learned a lot of things about the bridge and what is on the other side, so *there*." Randolph tried to fold his arms across his chest to demonstrate his annoyance, but his arms were too short to pull it off, so he just made a face at Bits and let it go at that.

Miss Maya had a droopy face, downturned eyes, a bit of a sniffle and the beginnings of tears. She was as sad as sad could be, at least for the time being. Her two best friends were squabbling and it was her fault. She was just about to get more teary when she got an idea. Maybe if she let Bits carry Randolph, she would feel safer. After all, she would be defended by a fierce, if rather small, bear. Miss Maya remembered the time when Bits hurt her toe on a rock and cried. She gave Randolph to her to hold and he knew just what to say and do to make Bits feel better.

"I'll tell you what Bits," said Miss Maya. "I will let you carry Randolph so you can protect him, since he is small and easily stepped on, meanwhile, I will keep a sharp look out for anything trying to attack us and gobble us up."

Bits agreed and Miss Maya handed Randolph over to her. She knew it was the right thing to do, but she wasn't so sure that without Randolph she would be brave enough to go forward. Their fighting behind them, Bits and Randolph were now the best of friends. Randolph found a comfortable spot at the bend of her elbow and snuggled into it. They were now ready for the adventure. Miss Maya seemed to hesitate and fidget about with her feet.

"Come on, mayonnaise, let's get moving," chided Bits.

With a newfound determination Miss Maya surged forward and started to cross the bridge with Bits and Randolph close behind. The bridge was not very long and yet it seemed to take them forever to cross it. It was as if the bridge grew longer as they went forward.

At long last they were across the bridge. The landscape seemed, at first, to be the same as on their end of the bridge, but as they watched, it began to change. Green grass appeared instead of sand and rock. They saw trees of all sorts and there were soft, puffy, white clouds in the sky that moved leisurely along, casting shadows as they passed. Off in the distance they saw something moving towards them. They couldn't tell what it was at first but as it got closer, they saw that it was a very old man sitting on the back of a donkey. He wore a flowing robe with stars all over it and a pointed hat with dragons on it. He had a long white beard and his hair was also white.

"Who are you?" Bits stammered.

"I am the great magician Marlin," said the old man.

"Don't you mean Merlin?" asked Miss Maya. "I think a marlin is some sort of fish."

"I know that it says Merlin in all of the storybook legends, but I changed it to Marlin so I wouldn't get so much junk mail from insurance companies, book clubs, time shares, and coupons for stuff I do not want or need," said Marlin. "I am here for a couple of reasons. The first reason being that this time of year England is very soggy and cold which isn't good for my old bones. The second reason is that I am feeling a presence here that is hostile and dangerous. I will need to use some spells and several of my crystals to sort it out."

"Well, Mr. Magician Marlin, I hope you can sort it out soon," said Miss Maya, feeling anxious but trying not to show it, so she changed the subject instead. "We have never been to this side of the bridge before so we are new here. With trees and grass appearing, we don't know where anything is. Can you show us around a little?"

"Of course, of course," said Marlin. "But first tell me how you got here."

"We came across the Bridge to Everywhere," said Miss Maya.

"My, my, my," said Marlin, "there seems to be a rather large problem."

"A problem?" said Randolph, sniffling a bit. "Does that mean you are going to gobble us up?" asked Randolph in a shaky voice.

"No, no little bear," replied Marlin. "If you had come across the Bridge to Somewhere it could be very bad. There are some pretty mean gobblers over that way. The problem is that I don't see any sort of bridge at all. Not even a single board or stick, so yes, a problem."

The girls and Randolph looked back to where the bridge was supposed to be. There was no trace of a bridge. This turn of events was too much for two little girls and a very small bear. They began to get teary-eyed.

"Now, now," said Marlin. "I can help you. This is something that can be fixed. You must stand in a circle, hold hands, and close your eyes. It's okay if Randolph can't touch the ground with his feet, as long as he is part of the circle. You will hear some funny sounds but, whatever you do, do not open your eyes until I tell you to do so."

The girls and Randolph stopped sniffling and did what Mr. Magician Marlin said. They heard some sort of mumbling that sounded like Grandpa when he said a prayer. After what seemed like a long time Marlin told them to open their eyes. When they did, they saw the bridge right where it had been before. They could even hear Miss Maya's mom calling them to come in for a snack.

"Mr. Marlin, you really are a great magician," said Miss Maya. "We have to go now but we will come back at a later time."

"Or maybe we won't," said Bits and Randolph at the same time.

"Well, if you do come back, I will be waiting for you, and we will have many wonderful adventures together," said Marlin.

"Ah, if it wouldn't be too much to ask, could you check under the bridge before we come back?" asked Randolph. "We want to be sure there's nothing under there that might gobble us up. If you see anything like that, could you magic it away to the moon or something?"

"Don't worry little bear, I won't let anything gobble you up," said Marlin. "What puzzles me is what happened to the bridge in the first place. I sense magic not of my making. I will think this over."

With that assurance the three of them dashed for the bridge. When they looked back to wave at Marlin, neither he nor his donkey were anywhere to be seen.

CHAPTER 2

MISS MAYA AND THE HEALING OF RANDOLPH

"Well, hello my young friends," said Marlin who had just more or less materialized on the safe side of the bridge some time later. "I am very glad to see all of you again."

"We are also happy to see you," said Miss Maya. "We have been very worried about what you said about a dangerous and hostile presence. Have you learned anything more about it?"

"In one way I have, but in another way, I have not," said the magician. "I have been able to divine that there is a definite presence here. Unfortunately, the nature of the presence is carefully protected by some very powerful spells. I can only tell you that the presence is very old, and it does not come from the spirit realm. For now, there is nothing we can do except be watchful."

"That is very scary, Mr. Marlin," said Miss Maya.

"Isn't there something that we can do?" said Bits.

"Well, there are some things, such as charms. I will now give some to each one of you," said Mr. Magician Marlin. He gave the girls and Randolph some small metal charms on beat-up old bracelets. They looked vaguely like dragons that had been ill-used. "Other than that, the best defense is to keep your wits about you, don't go out at night, and wherever you go, go together. There is strength in numbers. Also, there is strength in a nap, and I need one so that we can get on with this adventure. I will see all of you on the other end of the bridge in a little while after I have had time to recharge my batteries."

"Well, hmmm, I don't know," said Randolph, the one-eyed little bear. "Last time was okay. We weren't eaten or anything, but we might have been. If we go, someone should look under the bridge first to see if there is anything that looks hungry lurking about."

"Will you go if I look under the bridge first?" asked Miss Maya.

"Oh no, we can't risk you," said Randolph. "What if something jumps out and bites you, something like a snake or a salamander, what then?"

"So, I suppose that leaves me," said Bits in an angry voice. "I guess you think that I am expendable. Who cares if Bits gets bitten or eaten? Well I am not going to do it, so just get your furry butt across the bridge and not another word about it."

At this Randolph started to sniffle and hung his head.

"Crying is okay, but do it quietly if you must," said Bits.

"Now, now Bits, don't be so hard on Randolph," said Miss Maya. "He is brave in his own way, or at least as much as he needs to be. Besides he only sees half of the world since he only has one eye, which is my fault since they tell me that I chomped it off when I was teething as a baby."

With the matter settled, the trio started across the bridge. Miss Maya wondered if Mr. Magician Marlin actually had batteries to keep him going. Sometimes she wondered if grown-ups actually told things straight or if they bent them a little. Bits and Randolph shot dagger glances at each other as they proceeded. Miss Maya saw their antics and told them both to stop it. Bits said that Randolph was a scaredy-cat with Randolph pointing out that he was a bear and not a cat and that he only had one eye. This last comment did not seem to impress Bits much. Just then they heard a hearty voice greet them from the far end of the bridge.

"It seems that you are not all happy about this adventure," said Mr. Magician Marlin, rubbing the sleep from his eyes and struggling to his feet. "If my hearing is working, the problem seems to have something to do with Randolph having his eye bitten off by Miss Maya when she was too little to know any better. I can fix that if you will let me. What do you say Randolph?"

"Well, umm, yes, well, err, can you really fix my eye Mr. Magician Marlin?" asked Randolph.

"Yes, I can," said Marlin. "However, the problem isn't so much fixing your eye, since you don't seem to have an eye on the left side of your face. Instead, I can give you a brand new one.

Would you like a brand new left eye Randolph?"

"Oh yes, yes I would," said Randolph in a very excited voice. "Please give me a new left eye Mr. Magician Marlin. I would be so very grateful to you if you could do it."

"Very well," said Marlin. "You must listen very carefully and do exactly as I say. Your two friends will need to help you. You will hear some very strange sounds, some of them may be very loud. All of you must close your eyes and do not open them until I tell you to do so. It may be a little bit scary; can you all do that?"

Bits and Miss Maya both nodded their heads vigorously yes. They were instructed to form a circle holding hands or, in the case of Randolph, whatever passed for hands. When they had done this, Marlin walked a short distance away and reached up like he was getting something from a shelf. A very large, old book appeared in his hand out of thin air with OBSTIPESCERES ET CARMENS in block letters on the cracked leather front cover.

Marlin shuffled through the book, looked up and told them to keep holding hands and to close their eyes and to not let go of each other until he told them to do so. When all was ready, he began to chant in a very loud voice, "*TE ROGAMUS OMNIPOTENS DEUS COGNASCIT DEUM. SED ET HOC PARUM BONUS NOVUS PARIES OCULUM SINISTER URSUS PARVUS SANABIT.*"

He repeated this charm three times then told the children and one very frightened little bear to let go of each other's hands and open their eyes. When they did so, and after blinking in the bright light for a bit, they saw that Randolph was flat on his back on the bridge and not moving.

"Oh no," said Miss Maya and Bits at the same time.

"Is he dead Mr. Marlin?" asked Miss Maya.

"No, I am not dead," said Randolph. "At least I don't think I'm dead. Maybe I am since I can't see anything."

"You are not dead Randolph," said Marlin.

"But I can't see anything," said Randolph in a shaky voice.

"Open your eyes, fur face," said Bits. Randolph opened his eyes, plural this time, since he had a bright, shiny, little black eye in each socket.

"I can see! I can see everything!" cried a joyous Randolph.

The two girls ran up to Randolph and Mr. Magician Marlin and took turns hugging both of them. They both bounced up and down with joy, dizzy from happiness.

"Thank you, thank you, a million times, Mr. Magician Marlin! And thank you girls also, but I must ask you not to squeeze me too hard! I don't want my new eye to pop out," said Randolph.

Marlin picked up the book of spells and placed it upon the invisible shelf, causing it to disappear. He turned back to his little band of small admirers. "I don't know about all of you, but this magic and sorcery have made me very hungry," said Mr. Magician Marlin. "Why don't we have a picnic in the woods?"

"That is a very good idea, but we don't have any food, also there aren't any woods, this being a desert and all," said Miss Maya in response to Marlin. He winked at her mischievously.

"I believe you saw my donkey the last time I was here," said Marlin. "But I didn't introduce him to you. His name is Tamad."

"Come over here and meet our new friends, Tamad," said Marlin. At this point, out of nowhere, there appeared a very scruffy donkey loaded down with saddle bags hanging nearly to the ground on both sides of the tired looking beast. Tamad shuffled forward and presented his forehead to each of the children and the small bear, who had to be lifted to pet him. The formalities thus completed, Marlin lead the way over a rise, panting only a little from the steepness of the slope. On the other side they saw a forest that stretched to the horizon. Marlin picked his way along a path in the forest until they came to a meadow of green grass, scattered yellow flowers, chirping birds, and a small gurgling stream.

"If you two young ladies would be so kind as to empty the saddle bag on Tamad's right side, I will lay everything out. Afterward, please lift off the saddle bag on his left side so he can graze in the meadow. Then we will eat," said Marlin. Their hunger-driven response was nearly instantaneous.

The girls had never seen a picnic such as this before. There were sandwiches, hot dogs, fried chicken, pizza, and hamburgers cooked to perfection and steaming hot. There were potato chips, potato salad, and Cheetos. The watermelon and ice cream were both ice cold and delicious. Nowhere was there even a hint of spinach, carrots, broccoli or other horrible foods and nothing tasted of sulfur. They ate until they were ready to burst.

"Wow! Mr. Magician Marlin, we never thought we would ever see so much food in one place in our entire lives," said Miss Maya after a rather large, unlady-like belch.

Even Randolph chowed down. He waved a chicken leg in the air with a big smile on his face. Suddenly he looked worried.

"Do bears eat chicken?" he asked in a timid voice.

"It certainly looks like they do," said Bits.

With a wave of his wand Marlin set all of the dishes flying through the air. They passed into and out of the stream and ended up in Tamad's saddle bags, sparkling clean. "Now then," said Marlin, "you all need to head home so your mothers don't worry. I have to go to Kansas to see about a girl named Dorothy and some witches." He sighed. "A wizard's work is never done. Before I go, there are some important things that you need to know," said Marlin. "Adults can't see wizards, but they can see those humbugs in the circus who call themselves wizards but can't coax flour out of a paper bag. They can't see things done by magic, so even though Randolph has a new eye, the eye will not be visible to adults. If you tell them about the magic I've done today in the forest, they will not believe you and might say that you are just making it up. It is best to say you were playing near Grandpa's bridge, which is the truth, and let it go at that. It would be a good idea if you both volunteered to take a nap. I will rub some magic powder on your foreheads so you can easily fall asleep," and he proceeded to do so.

Then he whistled for Tamad and struggled his way onto the back of the donkey, in the way of an old man. Marlin jiggled the reins and Tamad began his slow shuffle forward. Over his shoulder Marlin shouted a goodbye which was returned by the girls. The next thing they knew, they stood by Grandpa's bridge, which they proceeded to cross.

"That was a great adventure," said Bits. "I hope we can do it again soon if Randolph doesn't rat us out to your mom."

"Not only can grownups not see magicians or real magic, they can't talk to or hear little brown bears. I don't know about you guys, but I feel sleepy. I think I'll take Marlin's advice," said Miss Maya.

And so, they parted for now to get ready for their next adventure of magic, and the care of a small brown bear who was just a little bit braver than he was this morning.

CHAPTER 3

THE DEMON GUSION GETS INVOLVED

While our young friends had their adventure, in a city far away but still part of the United States, George Gusion, the owner of Old Spanish Trial Ventures, suddenly looked up from the pile of papers on his desk. *Something is wrong,* he thought. *There is something going on out west, something that is not part of the plan and I don't like it. If I don't like it, the master will most certainly not like it either. The consequences could be bad, very bad.* He picked up the phone on his desk.

"Iris, I want you to find Glaysa Labolis and have him come here at once. Don't ask questions, just do it. If he makes a fuss tell him that this is Priority Alpha so that he doesn't stop off for ice cream on the way."

"Yes sir, at once," said Iris, the messenger of the demons. While he was waiting, Gusion, a member of Legion 40 with the rank of Duke among the demons, tried to focus on the dusty little desert town where the trouble had started all those years ago. It came slowly, but he eventually remembered the two old geezers who tried to build a magical bridge using two of their ancient grimoires to help them to do it. They had no standing in the angelic or demonic realms so they were trying to string various pieces of knowledge together from whatever sources seemed reasonable. They soon found that information from the internet was often poorly researched, fanciful, generally unreliable, and full of gaps and nonsense. After fiddling with and cursing their computers, they gave up on electronic media and struck out on their own. They both had elements of a classical education, so things like Latin and Greek were only moderately difficult. When they tried to go back further than was covered in their grimoires they ran headlong into Sumerian texts, which they had no clue how to decipher and thus their studies ended. That was where Gusion came in and helped the ungrateful old geezers along. At first, they were properly grateful, but it didn't take them long to get very full of themselves and to begin prancing around and showing off. They were warned. They ignored the warning. They paid the price.

CHAPTER 4

MISS MAYA AND THE CONDOR

Miss Maya, Bits, and Randolph played on the Bridge to Everywhere. There was a good deal of teasing and more than a little giggling. Suddenly, a large shadow passed over them. Startled, all three looked up. They saw a very large bird flying not high overhead.

"What on earth is that?" asked Bits.

"It looks like the biggest bird in the world, it looks very scary, and it looks very hungry," said Randolph in a frightened voice. "I don't like the looks of it one bit. Do you know what it is, Miss Maya?"

"I have no idea what sort of bird it is. Also, I don't know if it eats children," replied Miss Maya.

"What about small bears?" said Randolph with a quivering voice. "Do you think that it eats small bears?"

"Oh, I am sure it would love to gobble up a small bear, especially since the small ones are the most tender," said Bits.

"But—but—but, I have claws and sharp teeth so wouldn't the bird be afraid of hurting its stomach if it ate me?" said Randolph on the verge of either tears, fainting, or both.

"I think you have too many buts, and I think that the bird would think of you as a delicacy and gobble you up in a second," said Bits.

"Oh no," said Randolph. Thereupon, he started running around in circles, waving his stubby arms in the air, shaking and trembling in the process.

"Stop it, Bits. Can't you see how you're frightening poor Randolph? You should be ashamed of yourself for scaring him like that," said Miss Maya. Still looking up, "That huge bird is flying in circles over us."

"It seems to be watching us more and more. I don't like this one bit. I wish that Mr. Marlin the Magician was here; he would probably know about this rotten bird," answered Bits. There was a popping sound, the air seemed to shimmer and waver, and there was Mr.

Magician Marlin standing at the far end of the Bridge to Everywhere. With the addition of a suddenly-appearing magician, complete with a popping noise, Randolph made a sound somewhere between a sob and a wail and dove under the bridge.

"Come out of there you coward," yelled Bits. "Mr. Magician Marlin is here to help us find out about the big bird."

"I don't care what kind of bird it is," said Randolph. "I am not coming out from under the bridge until that bird is gone."

"I thought you were afraid that something hungry for small bears might be under the bridge," said Miss Maya.

"I don't see anything drooling or snapping in a hungry sort of way," said Randolph. "So, I am going to stay right here until that bird goes away so far that we can't see it anymore."

"Well," said Marlin the Magician, "I think I can solve the mystery, a little bit, anyway. The rather large bird flying around in circles appears to be a condor. There are not many of them around here anymore. They are seen from time to time in this area but are more common to the north. They have them in South America in the Andes mountains. The Andean condors have smaller bodies but longer wings than the California condor. I guess it might be a wandering albatross, however, those birds almost never get this far north. Also, their wings, while longer than a California condor, are quite narrow. Did I leave anything out?"

"No, Mr. Magician Marlin, I think you gave us way more information than we need to know," said Bits. Just then and for no apparent reason, the very large bird, now known to be a California condor, swooped down to the ground and then back into the air. "Get down, he picked up a rock," said Bits.

The two girls curled up into balls with their hands over their heads and their eyes squeezed closed. Nothing seemed to happen so, after a while, they got up, dusted off, and looked around. Everything seemed the same. Then they noticed that Mr. Magician Marlin was lying on the ground, out like a light.

"I know that he is very old," said Bits, "but this is a fine time to take a nap since he just finished one."

"How old do you think he is?" asked Miss Maya.

"He could be as old as forty," replied Bits.

Just then the huge bird swooped down and grabbed Miss Maya and started to fly away, getting higher and higher with each stroke of its very large wings. Mr. Magician Marlin suddenly sat up.

"That rock knocked me out," said Mr. Magician Marlin. "Where is Miss Maya?"

"The big bird took her," sobbed Bits, pointing to the large bird that was getting smaller and smaller.

"This is terrible," said Mr. Magician Marlin. "I will try a turnaround spell." Whereupon he began to chant and wave his arms toward the condor. Nothing happened.

"I will try to establish a link to Miss Maya so that she can tell us what she is seeing and help us to rescue her," said the magician. He began chanting a something or other that consisted of all sorts of strange words and sounds. "I have a link! She sounds very relieved to hear from us. I will let you hear what she is telling me."

"Mr. Magician Marlin," came the distant voice of a very frightened little girl. "I don't know where we are, but the bird is flying towards a mountain."

"When you look down, what do you see?" asked Mr. Magician Marlin.

"The ground is very flat and there is a large, almost round, circle. Like a lake but no swimming," was the reply.

"Anything else?" asked Mr. Magician Marlin.

"Yes," came the trembling voice of Miss Maya. "I see a something like a snake on the ground that is very long, dusty and dry. No fishing."

"It sounds like she is describing a dry lake and a dry river," said Mr. Magician Marlin.

"We need to rescue her," said Bits between sobs. "But, how can we? She is up in the air and flying away from us. Please help her, Mr. Magician Marlin."

"We will get Miss Maya back," said Marlin. "What we need is something we can ride on and something that is very fast." There was some head scratching and eye scrunching on the part of Mr. Magician Marlin. Then he opened his eyes wide, snapped his fingers and said, "We need a griffin."

"What is a griffin?" asked Bits.

"A griffin is a supposedly mythical creature that has been part of the history of the Middle East and Europe for centuries. It has the hind legs, tail, and back of a lion with the head, wings, and front legs of an eagle. It can fly very fast, for a long distance, and is a very fierce fighter," said Mr. Magician Marlin.

"Where can we get one?" asked Bits. "I haven't seen any place that has a sign saying, 'Rent a Griffin.'"

"You are right, there are no such places. We have to conjure one," said Mr. Magician Marlin.

"How do we do that?" asked Bits.

"There are two ways to do it," replied Mr. Magician Marlin. "One way is to use several, complicated spells that require different things that are sometimes very hard to come by. The other way to do it is to use something that already exists and change it into a griffin. This method is much quicker and simpler, but we need someone or something that is willing to be changed into a griffin."

"That means that it will be either me or Randolph," said Bits. "I think Randolph would be best."

"I heard that," said a faint voice under the bridge. "I don't want to be a grifink or any other such creature. I like being a little brown bear just fine, thank you very much."

"Randolph," said Bits. "Ms. Maya is in very deep trouble and we are the only ones that can get her out of it with the help of Mr. Magician Marlin. Besides, the griffin is very powerful and strong.

Wouldn't you like to be powerful and strong instead of a scared kitty cat?"

"I told you before, I am a bear and not a kitty cat. I am proud of being a bear. I don't want to spend the rest of my life as a grifink. So there," said Randolph.

"First of all, Randolph, it is a griffin and not a grifink. Secondly, you would only have to be a griffin until we get Miss Maya back and then I can change you back to your current self. You would probably be a griffin for only a few hours," said Mr. Magician Marlin.

"I want Miss Maya back very badly, but I think I will just stay under the bridge until she comes back on her own," said Randolph.

"Now you listen here, Randolph," said a very angry Bits, "She can't be saved without our help so get your dusty, furry butt up here so we can get her back or I will ask Mr. Magician Marlin to turn you into a turnip or a toad or something equally unpleasant."

"Well, okay, I guess, err, I mean, well, it doesn't hurt or anything like that, does it, Mr. Magician Marlin?" said a very shaky little bear.

"It won't hurt," said Mr. Magician Marlin. "In fact, you will feel great strength and power."

"Okay, then, I guess I will do it," said Randolph, "but if it gets to hurting I am going to leave."

"Very well, the choice is made," said Mr. Magician Marlin as he reached underneath his robe and brought out a bottle of a silvery liquid that seemed to slowly move around in the bottle as if it was alive.

"I am going to pour some of this liquid over your head and body Randolph," said Mr. Magician Marlin. "It will feel cool but not cold and will get you ready for the change. It will make your body tingle like your foot does if you sit on it for too long."

"Randolph, I just want you to know that no matter how much I squabble with and tease you, that I am very proud of you right now," said Bits.

"Nod your head Randolph if you are ready to go ahead with it," said Mr. Magician Marlin.

Randolph reluctantly nodded his head. Nothing happened for a minute or so, after which the process of change began.

"You and Bits need to close your eyes and don't open them until I tell you to. By now you should both be used to the chanting and noise," said Mr. Magician Marlin. There followed a long, drawn out chanting and even what seemed like a choir singing. Some of it was very loud and some so soft it could barely be heard. None of it was in a language that either Randolph or Bits had ever heard before. After what seemed like an eternity, Mr. Magician Marlin told them to open their eyes. They both did so.

Bits was so startled with what she saw that her legs shook violently and she almost fainted. There standing where Randolph had been was a large, strong-appearing, brown-coated animal with large wings that was looking at her with surprised eyes.

"Can he talk?" said Bits.

"Yes, he can, but it won't sound anything like his regular voice, so don't be frightened. Please remember that this is a new experience for him also, and it takes some time to get the change straight in his mind as well as yours," said Mr. Magician Marlin.

"My name is now Anzu," said a deep voice coming from the griffin. "Those who look upon me know fear and tremble at my might. You would do well to do likewise."

Bits had no trouble at all doing likewise.

It was obvious that they would have to act quickly to be able to rescue Miss Maya. Rather than a long debate they both jumped on Anzu's back and headed out in the general direction of the condor carrying Miss Maya. Even though the griffin was weighed down a bit with his passengers he was making pretty good time. They soon caught up enough to spot the condor in the distance. It was obvious that the condor was headed for the rather large mouth of a cave in the mountain. It soon darted into the cave and could no longer be seen. The griffin was rapidly closing in on the condor and soon the condor and the griffin were inside of a sizable cave. The condor dropped Miss Maya in front of a scraggily looking old woman and promptly departed. When Anzu stopped inside of the cave, the passengers promptly dismounted. None of them complained about inflight snacks, lack of an inflight movie, or foot rests as they scrambled to the floor of the cave.

The old hag, called Niviane, held Miss Maya in a rather tight grip. Miss Maya didn't say anything, she just looked rather dazed by all of the day's happenings to this point.

CHAPTER 5

MISS MAYA AND THE WITCH

"**P**ut her down and do so at once," shouted Mr. Magician Marlin.

"My, my, Merlin," said Niviane. "Is that any way to greet an old friend? We haven't seen each other for over 1,500 years and now you're yelling at me? Such manners you have. Didn't King Arthur teach you anything while you were his lapdog? If you want this puny little mortal, you can have her. She was only bait to get you here so that I can kill you properly." Where upon she placed Miss Maya at Marlin's feet and backed away. A wizard's duel was inevitable and Niviane started it off by throwing a large ball of fire at Marlin, which he dodged. The ball of flame went out of the entrance of the cave.

"Is that all that you've got?" Mr. Magician Marlin said as he blasted Niviane with a huge boxing glove that knocked her down. She twisted sharply, throwing a lightning bolt straight at Marlin, who leapt to the side. The bolt tried to cut through his robe but couldn't and fizzled harmlessly to the ground in a shower of sparks that fell short of Miss Maya. The two threw lightning bolts, fire balls, and whirligigs at each other to very little general effect, other than to make the cave smell horribly of sulphur.

With his feints and shifts and carefully aimed bolts of fire, Marlin had worked Niviane towards the back of the cave. All the while Miss Maya had not moved. Bits and Anzu couldn't tell if she was or wasn't breathing. Now, however, she began to stir. Without be told, the griffin started edging toward Miss Maya who was no longer at the center of the duel. Niviane was so busy trying to best Marlin that she didn't see what was happening with Miss Maya. Anzu reached Miss Maya and lowered himself until he was flat on the floor of the cave. In a low rumbly voice, he told Miss Maya to get on his back, which she did after a brief struggle.

Marlin and Bits made a run for the griffin. Marlin sent a bolt of sizzling energy over his shoulder, so strong that it electrified the air enough for everyone's hair to stand on end. Marlin's hair and beard were charged to the point that they looked like he had just gone through the fluff cycle of the dryer. When the bolt hit the roof of the cave over the witch's position it caved in and sent the rocks crashing down on her. She tried to reverse the spell but was too late and was buried under several tons of rock.

Marlin and Bits jumped on the back of the griffin behind Miss Maya. Anzu made a running start and leapt into the air just as they shot out of the cave. At first, they descended rapidly. Anzu flapped his wings as hard as he could, and they rose up and flew away with Marlin and the two girls holding on to each other and the fur of Anzu. They cried out of happiness for the terrible fate that they had narrowly escaped. They touched down gently by the bridge and the girls and Marlin got off. As soon as they were off of Anzu's back he began to shake and cough and then there was a bunch of smoke. As the smoke fade, they saw a very puzzled and shaky little brown bear.

"What happened?" said Randolph. "I dreamed of flying and then there was fire and explosions, but I feel okay," said Randolph.

"Mr. Magician Marlin, who was that awful person?" asked Miss Maya. "Is she dead? Will she be back?"

"No to your second question, but I am not sure about the answer to your third question," said Marlin. "As to your first question, I have known Niviane for around 1,500 years, give or take, and allowing for leap years. I thought that she was dead, but I guess not. Those rocks that fell on her were very big and there were lots of them. She was well trained in magic and is very clever; I should know since I trained her, but that is a story for another time. I want to leave you three very well protected from evil."

CHAPTER 6

THE ARRIVAL OF PEGASUS

The girls played on the far side of the bridge, prancing and jumping around in their leggings and T-shirts on a warm autumn day. There was a good deal of giggling and downright laughter. Even Randolph joined in the fun, although chasing him about wasn't much of a challenge, since with his short, stumpy legs he could not run very fast, so he was easy to catch. He was also fun to tickle since he laughed without holding back.

Just then a shadow passed over the girls and Randolph causing them all to look up.

"Not again," said Bits. "Haven't we had enough of magic and such for now?"

"Do I need to dive under the bridge again?" asked Randolph with nervousness in his voice.

"You can if you want Randolph, if it will make you feel better," said Miss Maya. "But it looks like our visitor is Mr. Magician Marlin and he is riding on the back of a horse with wings. It doesn't look like a griffin though."

"Well it had better not be a griffin since I am the only griffin in these parts!" said a semi-belligerent Randolph.

"Randolph, it sounds like you have been watching too many western movies. Next thing you know you'll be wearing a gun, which is way too heavy for you, and a cowboy hat, which would be so big that it would be down around your ankles. We would have to cut eye holes in it so you could see out," said Bits.

With that the winged horse and rider came to a stop in a small cloud of dust in front of the girls and Randolph.

"Mr. Magician Marlin, what a surprise it is to see you," said Miss Maya. "What a beautiful horse you have! What is his name, and is it a he or she?"

"This is the winged horse Pegasus from ancient Greece," said Mr. Magician Marlin. "He did several things way back then, some of which were very dangerous. So now he helps me get around when my old donkey Tamad isn't quite up to the trip. You can pet him if you like."

The girls both did so, lifting up Randolph so he could join in. "It is okay if you give him some grass. He is partial to carrots but please don't give him an apple since all sorts of mischief and misery were brought about via poisoned apples, golden apples, and any other sorts of apples, including apple sauce. As a result, he is very afraid of apples. But that is not why I stopped by just now. I was getting an uneasy feeling in my stomach, which usually means that something is amiss. So, I thought I would take a look at the cave where Niviane is trapped and I saw something disturbing."

If Marlin the Magician was troubled, the girls were downright terrified and poor Randolph was rigid with fear. For a while no one spoke. The only sound was Pegasus shuffling his hooves in the dirt.

"What was it that you saw Mr. Magician Marlin?" asked Miss Maya in a subdued voice.

"I noticed a crude circle drawn in the dirt outside of the cave. In the circle were several yellow candles and the scent of rosemary in the air. I also remembered that Niviane has a golden ring on her left hand," said Mr. Magician Marlin.

The two girls looked at each other with puzzled expressions on their faces, while Randolph scrambled under the bridge. Fortunately for him there was nothing hungry lurking under there to gobble him up.

"Do the circle, the yellow candles, the gold ring, and the smell of rosemary mean anything special?" asked Miss Maya.

"I am afraid that it might, Miss Maya," sighed Marlin. "Those are the sigils associated with the demon Glasya-Labolas. The sigils are used to summon the demon and to make requests for his aid. He is not to be thought of as a good spirit, although he can be. He will do anything to help a friend. He was cast out of heaven when the angels rebelled, and it appears that he caused a great deal of difficulty while doing so and was further cast out of the demonic ranks. He took it very badly since he didn't think that it was his fault and has held a grudge ever since. He can appear in demon form, like a large dog with a griffin's wings, or in human form as a young man with short blond hair and white wings.

"Is he dangerous to us?" asked Miss Maya. "Did we do something to make him mad so that he might want to hurt us?" This last was accompanied by a whimpering sound from under the bridge. Mr. Magician Marlin stood stock still with his head down fiddling with his long white beard.

"I am afraid that the answer, at least partially, is yes, although it pains me to give you this information," said Mr. Magician Marlin. "I have heard rumors that he has done some rather bad things at the request of Niviane. That could mean that she might ask for his help in dealing with us. He is known to have a violent temper when he is upset and his rage can be fearful. On the other hand, he can use the great power at his command to do good. He can teach almost anything to his friends and can generate love and good feelings between his friends and even his enemies, depending on the mood he is in. But the anger of Glasya-Labolas can be terrible indeed."

"If this Gladys Labony is so bad aren't there some angels who might protect us from him?" said Bits with a hopeful look.

"Bits! Be careful what you say. His name is Glasya-Labolas. Do not make fun of it or him, no matter what happens, no matter what he says or does. He has ears everywhere and could even be here right now, in his invisible form, listening to everything that we say and watching everything that we do. If you write something on a piece of paper he could instantly find out what it said, even if you burned up the paper and scattered the ashes. Say nothing that may be even slightly insulting. If you can't do that I may have to put a spell of silence on you which, if I am killed in the battle that might be to come, no one could take the spell off and you would never be able to speak again."

"Please Bits," said Miss Maya. "For all of our sakes think very carefully what you say. Just remember what the teacher told us last week. She said that silence is golden which is why there is so little of it. Is there something that we can do? Is there any hope for us Mr. Magician Marlin?"

"Yes, Miss Maya, I think that there might be. You have heard that sometimes it is best to fight fire with fire. In this case, demon magic with demon magic. We may need to summon one of our own. I need to think

on it. I will just stretch out here on the bridge for a short time and I am sure it will come to me." And off he went to lie and think.

"That thinking he is doing sounds a lot like snoring," said Bits.

"We have been the beneficiaries of his snoring in the past," said Miss Maya. "However, we seem to have survived it recently. We will have to wait until he is done with Glasya-Labolas before he gives us another serenade."

CHAPTER 7

COMES THE DEMON

Miss Maya and Bits fidgeted about waiting for Mr. Magician Marlin to wake up. They tried talking loudly, pacing about on the bridge, and stomping their feet. The loud snoring continued unabated.

"Maybe we should poke him with a stick," said Bits.

"Don't you dare, Bits. He is a famous magician who has been very nice to us. If you poke him with a stick he might turn you into a frog or something worse."

"So, what should we do, Miss Smarty Pants, stand around on this rotten old bridge until we are as old as Marlin?" said Bits.

"My grandfather built this bridge and it is not rotten. Besides, why are you calling me 'smarty pants?' You know I don't act like that, not even for a minute, but we both know that you have a mean mouth," said Miss Maya.

"That's not fair," said Bits with a distinct frown which included a wrinkled forehead. With a couple of snorts, a few coughs and throat clearing, Marlin sat up, rubbed his eyes, and looked around.

"I have never heard you two girls fight before, except for you, Bits, and that usually involves squabbling with Randolph," said Mr. Magician Marlin. "Something is going on here and I am afraid that I know what it is."

"I am sorry, Bits. I didn't want to be mean to you," said Miss Maya.

"I am sorry, too," said Bits. "You're my best friend in the whole world."

At this point the two girls gave each other teary, sniffily hugs. After that it was all over as if it had never happened.

"What did you mean, Mr. Magician Marlin. when you said you knew what was going on here?" asked Miss Maya.

"Do you remember when I scolded Bits about being careful what she says because a demon might hear her?" asked Marlin. "When you are looking for a sign that a demon is present, whether you can see it or not, argument and bickering can be an indicator of a demon skulking about. I can sense how fond you two are of each other and when I saw you trading insults I knew that something was very, very wrong."

You got that right, you old goat," said a handsome young man who had suddenly appeared. He had hair that was gold in appearance, a pair of white wings, designer jeans, plus a T-shirt that gave him the look of a buff teenager.

"So, you *are* here Glasya-Labolas. I imagine that Niviane summoned you," said Marlin. "Is she free or still pinned under the rocks?"

"A bit of both," said the demon. "The rocks are off of her as a result of our joint efforts, but she is pretty badly banged up to the point that it will take tincture of time and a large dollop of magic to make her a threat. She will probably never be her old self again."

"That is not all together bad, since there is a sizable piece of evil in her makeup," said Mr. Magician Marlin. "She can and does cause plenty of trouble if left to her own devices. If you look me up in the *Annals of Magic and Sorcery* you will see that she supposedly killed me a long time ago, 1,500 years, give or take, if my memory serves me right. I want to tell you up front that whatever quarrel you have with me is with me only and does not involve these young ladies. You have no grudge with them. In fact, Niviane used Miss

Maya as a carrot also, supposedly, to lure me to my doom. She was not successful and as a result of her evil, she ended up in the mess that she is in. I want your word that, whatever happens, you will not harm them."

"You would trust the word of a demon, Merlin? I am surprised. Maybe you are going soft in the head in your old age," said the demon.

"If you will keep track of your age, you will see that I am very much younger than you Glasya-Labolas, I am human—with certain enhancements—whereas you never were human which makes me quite different from you. For one thing, we humans physically age much faster than demons," replied Mr. Magician Marlin. "Further, you are one of the few demons that have been known to treat humans reasonably well, and to keep your word. I am asking you now that no matter what happens you will not only hold back from harming these girls, but will not allow harm to come to them."

"You have my word, but I cannot guarantee that another entity will not come forth and cripple or kill them," said the demon.

"Given your rank among the demons I doubt that any of them will try anything," said Marlin.

CHAPTER 8

THE BATTLE BEGINS

"Time to die Merlin," said the demon. The form of Glasya-Labolas began to shimmer, fade and brighten—very much like looking through heat waves. His form shook briefly and then was replaced by a large black dog with griffin wings. He gave a sinister growl and stalked toward Marlin. As the transformed Glasya-Labolas continued his slow approach, a whimpering sound came from under the bridge.

"Mr. Magician Marlin needs our help," said Miss Maya.

"Get your worthless, fuzzy butt up here Randolph. It's time to be a griffin again," said Bits, as she watched Glasya-Labolas preparing to pounce.

A shaky Randolph presented himself and Marlin poured the silvery liquid over him. The girls closed their eyes as soon as Marlin began his chant. There was the usual chanting noise and when it finished there was Anzu standing before them as before. Marlin motioned with his left hand for Anzu to come and stand beside him, which Anzu promptly did.

Glasya-Labolas leaped at Marlin and was greeted by a lightning bolt that made the air sizzle and smell of ozone with its passage. The newly brought forth demon leaped into the air high, enough for the lightning bolt to pass underneath him. Anzu jumped into the air also and flew straight at Glasya-Labolas who evaded him by performing a rolling dive while Anzu passed over him. Whereupon Glasya-Labolas rocketed upward, opened his mouth wide and tried to deliver a large bite out of Anzu. Marlin sent another lightning bolt, smaller this time, at Glasya-Labolas, which he had little trouble dodging, but which prevented Glasya-Labolas from biting Anzu.

The battle raged with the two griffins making passes at one another with each one trying to get the other by the throat but continuing to miss a mortal bite. Some of their biting and clawing landed on other parts of each griffin causing bits of fur and feathers to float downward. It soon became obvious that Glasya-Labolas's long experience with many battles by made him the better of the two warriors. Marlin was having trouble getting a clean shot at Glasya-Labolas with his fire balls. A small notebook appeared in Marlin's left hand and at the same time a pen showed up in his right hand. He wrote something in the note book and tossed it to Miss Maya. Glasya-Labolas made a diving grab at it, but Anzu landed hard on the back of Glaysa-Labolas, causing him to miss catching the notebook. Miss Maya grabbed it and opened it. A puzzled look crossed her face.

"Mr. Magician Marlin," said Miss Maya. "I can't make out the letters and words; they are in a strange language that I have never seen before."

"Sorry, Miss Maya," said Mr. Magician Marlin. "I forgot that they no longer teach the Assyrian language and Cuneiform writing in school anymore. Please hold the book open to the page where the writing is and put it out at arm's length from your body. It will feel warm in your hands. When the warmth is gone, read what is written on the page and follow the instructions which you should then be able to read."

Glasya-Labolas made another pass to get the book, outflanking Anzu in the process. Miss Maya dove to the ground with the book held firmly against her chest. Glasya-Labolas having too much speed and too little maneuvering room was close enough to Miss Maya for her to get a generous whiff of sulfur. He overshot her position and hit the ground with a glancing blow, digging a long ditch where he slid across the ground. Miss Maya scrambled up and went under the bridge, opened the book, and read what was written there. She stuck her hand out from under the bridge and waved at Mr. Magician Marlin to let him know that she had received and read the message.

Suddenly there was a small, soft voice in her head that she could tell was from Mr. Magician Marlin. "Miss Maya, we are slowly losing this battle. Anzu is new to this and even though he is fighting hard, he is not a seasoned veteran like Glasya-Labolas. We need a battle-hardened fighter. I know one who will fill the bill nicely. He is an angel named Briathos. Most angels have a specialty and his is stopping demons from doing bad things. He is very good at getting rid of demons or at least making them fail at whatever trouble that they are causing. The angels don't need all of the plants, metals, etc. that demons have as a sign which is theirs and theirs only, which can be a picture or their name written in Hebrew. In the case of Briathos, his sign is his name written in Hebrew which is: בְּדְדְתָאס"

Meanwhile, the battle between Glasya-Labolas and Anzu raged on with attacks and swooping moves on both sides. Anzu was being out-maneuvered more and more often and was just barely able to avoid a complete defeat. It was obvious that he could not hold out much longer.

CHAPTER 9

THE ARRIVAL OF THE ANGEL BRIATHOS

for the second time that day the air shimmered and with a popping noise there appeared a man covered with tattoos and a height of at least 8 feet. Tattoos were on his head and face as well as on his chest, back, and arms. He wore a pair of leather pants that fit him rather tightly. The tattoos glowed, his eyes shone, and he had a halo and wings. He looked the girls over and said, in a loud, deep voice, "Where is Merlin, and what is that pile of fur that looks like it has parts missing from it?"

Just then Mr. Magician Marlin appeared and said, "We are glad to see you Briathos. The one you are asking about is a small stuffed bear that I turned into a griffin named Anzu. He has defended us right well, but he has been fighting Glasya-Labolas. Even so, he gave all that he had to save us. Niviane brought Glasya-Labolas to kill us and he has nearly succeeded."

"I have dealt with that woman Niviane and Glaysa-Laabolas before," said Briathos. "They are not as tough as they think that they are, but together they can be a deadly nuisance."

Marlin filled Briathos in on what had happened up to this point and then the current state of affairs as well as he could. Before Briathos joined the battle, Marlin asked him to speak softly since his loud, deep angel voice usually caused headaches in mortals which, at this point, they didn't need.

"I am really glad that you are on our side, Mr. Angel Briathos," said Bits. Miss Maya agreed to that with vigorous nodding of her head.

Briathos sprang into the air and flapped his wings to gain altitude. With him joining the battle, a very tired griffin, who had collapsed in a pile of fur, began to stir. Miss Maya and Bits ran up to him and together dragged him below the bridge. When they saw how beat up he looked, both of the girls began to cry.

"I think he is going to die," said Bits.

"Oh no!" said Miss Maya. "Not Randolph."

"I don't think he is going to die right away," said Mr. Magician Marlin. "I have a magic potion that will help heal his wounds, even the ones that look pretty bad. Take this medicine and put it on the areas that are missing fur and have open wounds. It will sting him a bit which might make him twitch, so be careful that you do not get any of this on you since it could burn your mortal skin, all except your hands, which I have already protected with a spell.

When Briathos was high enough, he partly folded his wings close to his body and dove on Glaysa-Labolas, who had been circling the area to see what was happening. All the while Marlin was shooting fire balls at him. The first few made direct hits that caused Glasya-Labolas to let out some screams that were more like roars and, in either case, caused Marlin and the girls' ears to hurt. The demon and angel attacked each other, the demon using his clawed feet and fangs and the angel using his arms and legs in a Kung-Fu style of combat. The air was soon filled with falling hair and feathers along with screams, roars, and shouts. Having first tangled with Anzu, Glasya-Labolas was starting to show his fatigue. His turns were not as sharp and his speed was less than it had been. "Briathos, finish it," shouted Marlin.

The much-tattooed angel made a tight, circling climb so high that those on the ground could hardly see him. From the way that Glasya-Labolas was looking around it was obvious that he had lost track of Briathos. To regain any advantage that he had lost, he decided to take a hostage. He headed straight for

Miss Maya. Before he could get to her, a dark, blurred object bolted out of the sky straight as an arrow toward Glasya-Labolas. He didn't have time or altitude to put up any sort of meaningful defense.

"At the speed that he is going he will either kill himself and Glasya-Labolis or cause serious, difficult-to-heal damage to either or both of them," said Mr. Magician Marlin. Marlin's prophecy proved to be quite close to the truth. Briathos struck Glasya-Labolas a fearful blow, such that both of them plunged into the hard desert ground throwing up a huge cloud of dust and making a big hole. As the dust slowly cleared, Mr. Magician Marlin and the girls strained to see the combatants.

A hand appeared at the edge of the crater, followed by a head and a body. Even covered head to toe by a thick layer of dust, it was easy to see that the first to emerge from the crater was the angel Briathos. He dusted himself off as he walked over to the magician and his little friends. A dark blur appeared at the top of the crater and then vanished upward.

"What was that?" asked Miss Maya.

"That was the shadow of the demon Glasya-Labolas," said Briathos. "He is ashamed of me beating him and is trying to sneak off without anyone noticing. The most import thing is that he won't likely be back. He holds the rank of president in his legion but it is a rank without much attached to it. Most of it comes down to his own ego which he strokes quite often by wearing royal purple clothing."

Marlin finished the story that he had started with Briathos before the dust up. He brought him up to date concerning Niviane and his recent troubles with her, followed by the making of Randolph into a griffin, the appearance of Glasya-Labolas up to the point at which Marlin had summoned Briathos. "You are a very brave little bear. It is my pleasure to know you. Since this is the United States they don't give out knighthoods, but you deserve to be recognized for your valor," said Briathos. "Kneel down before me."

"Well, I am very much honored, but I don't have knees," said Randolph. The angel saw that what Randolph said was true. Briathos pulled his chin for a while and finally told Randolph to stand in from of him. Given the height of Randolph compared to that of Briathos it had the same effect as kneeling.

"Randolph, for your acts of bravery in the face of incredible danger, I hereby induct you into the Sacred Order of the Angelic Assistants."Whereupon he touched a sword to each shoulder causing Randolph to blush from head to toe, which wasn't easy to see given the general condition of his fur and his general overall dusty state. Briathos put a medal attached to a purple ribbon around Randolph's neck which, because of the honor given him, felt the greatest pride of his life. He positively glowed and couldn't stop smiling.

"Arise Angelic Assistant Randolph and go from here with your head held high." There was cheering from all around, even from some filmy shapes that quickly surrounded then and just as quickly disappeared. It had been a long day for two little girls and a very brave little bear who couldn't be happier.

"Have you anything to say Randolph?" said the angel.

"Ah, I mean—well—ah, will I have to go and fight again, say there is trouble and you need help from Anzu?"

"You have done well Randolph," said Mr. Magician Marlin. "There will be no need for you to fight. At least, that is the way that I see it. Briathos, whenever you are going to be near here let me know. We will have a glorious picnic. What do you say?"

"Thank you for your kind invitation," said Briathos. "As for your question Randolph, Merlin is more or less right, there is only a very small chance that you would be ordered to fight. However, if the order comes, you can't ignore it, don't even try. The consequences would be terrible. I have been getting hints on the angelic wavelength recently and I think that there was some activity years ago concerning your grandfather, Miss Maya. I will look through the Angelic Records, and if I find something important, we may all need to gather again." With that, Briathos vanished in a puff of smoke, and given his size, it was a rather large puff.

"We will try to do fun things, but you never know, Glaysa-Labolis and Niviane are a tricky lot," said Mr. Magician Marlin. "We must never let our guard down." As per usual, Mr. Magician Marlin vanished in his own puff of smoke.

With the departure of Briathos and Mr. Magician Marlin there was a lot of excited chatter between Miss Maya, Bits, and Randolph. They agreed that it was a great adventure and they also agreed that they didn't want to repeat it anytime soon, if ever.

"I just want to make something clear," said Randolph. "Since I am now an angelic assistant, I don't think I should be called fuzz butt or anything like that."

"Don't worry, Randolph," said Miss Maya. "We love and respect you. You have earned our faith in you and in your courage, even though sometimes it takes a bit before passing through. I hope Briathos can help us find out what happened to my grandfather."

CHAPTER 10

CARNIVAL IN TOWN

All of the participants, human and bear, in the fighting, brawling, and other various and sundry tricks and troubles were more or less in one piece despite their injuries which, on inspection, were less than they all had thought and well on the way to being healed.

After a week or two passed with no further angelic, demonic, magical or any other type of activity showing itself, the girls and the newly crowned Angelic Assistant Randolph had recharged their batteries and were ready for further adventure. They tried to summon Mr. Magician Marlin with no success. However, after a few more days of pouting and stomping about, they heard a faint, far away voice that sounded like Mr. Magician Marlin talking from the bottom of a barrel.

"Please forgive me," said the distant voice. "I have been trying to clean out a nest of nasty vampires. They are a difficult lot to deal with and most unpleasant. However, I should be done with them in another day or so and can then visit you."

"We will be happy to see you, Mr. Magician Marlin," said Miss Maya. Bits and the Angelic Assistant jumped up and down to show their happiness and enthusiasm.

The girls and Randolph said goodbye to Mr. Magician Marlin and eagerly awaited his visit.

Another week passed and then another. The playing and giggling around the bridge was much less spirited and the play times were of shorter duration. Miss Maya moped around the house and sighed most pitifully when she was near her mom's hearing.

Her mother, Naomi, was in her early thirties, short of stature, with brownish-black hair, a pretty face, and a trim figure with fashionable, but not extravagant, clothing. She taught English and Literature at the local high school. Miss Maya's father, Ralph, was two years older than Miss Maya's mother. He was of medium build, muscular, but not to the extent of looking like a gym rat. He had sandy-blond hair and an easy smile.

He worked as an electrician and was always trying to invent something. He dressed casually, occasionally wearing a neck tie, but couldn't stand the wretched thing and would only wear one when forced to do so, usually by Miss Maya's mother.

"Maya, what's the matter with you? You have such a long face, you look like your head is coming to a point. Are you and Bits fighting? You seem to get on with Randolph well enough, even though only you and Bits can communicate with that beat-up stuffed little bear—which is more than a little disturbing in and of itself. I saw in today's paper that there is a carnival in town, maybe we can take you and Bits to see it."

"Gee Mom, that would be great," said Miss Maya. "Let me call Bits and see if she can go with us."

"There *is* one catch," said Miss Maya's mom. "Charley will want to go and I don't want you squabbling with him. He will probably want to take his friend, George. So, if this is to happen, there has to be a peace treaty between all of you. You will be expected to act like proper young ladies and gentlemen. If there is any quarreling then you will all walk home."

"But Mom," said Miss Maya. "It's three or four miles from here to the carnival."

"Exactly," said Miss Maya's mom. "Do you agree with these terms and conditions?"

"I will agree if Charley does," said Miss Maya in an unhappy voice.

"Okay," said Miss Maya's mom. "I will call Bits's mom and if it's okay with her, with the same conditions, we can go this coming Saturday."

Miss Maya suddenly felt her mood and spirits elevate. She found Charley and gave him the good news. Charley was twelve years old. He was just slightly taller than Miss Maya. He had unruly blond hair which, from the look of it, had never seen the business side of a comb. He was rather typical for a boy of his age; scruffy clothes, scuffed shoes, and an aversion to having his hair cut, all of this leading to his feral appearance. His friend George was not quite a carbon copy of Charley. In height and build they were quite similar, except that George, being a year older, was a bit more solid than Charley. While Charley had blond hair, his friend George's hair bordered on dark brown. Otherwise, their dress was nearly identical and similarly disheveled. At this time in their lives, the two boys were not interested in anything historical, and they tended to narrow the range of their interests to chasing each other, wrestling, reading Manga, and playing video games.

They only slightly shared any of the interests of their sisters, preferring to think of them as "dumb girls" who were no fun to play with since they only wanted to play with their dolls. In a good old fashion rough house, the girls always ended up crying and telling their moms, which usually led to the boys getting a righteous scolding and some unpleasant chores to do.

With agonizing slowness Saturday eventually rolled around. Once the summit of the mothers had taken place and the four children had agreed to the terms of the peace treaty, the mothers made each of them turn in a complete circle, one at a time, to be sure that no one was keeping their fingers crossed which would, as is well known, negate the treaty.

When everyone, except Randolph (who doesn't have fingers) swore that they would honor the agreement they all piled into the car and headed for the carnival.

CHAPTER 11

THE HAUNTED HOUSE

After a sort of dust up with the jerk running the ferris wheel, the boys insisted on going to the haunted house which was only three venues down from the ferris wheel.

The girls and Randolph thought better of going into the haunted house since it didn't look all that scary, even though it did have a certain air of dust and mold about it such that lung damage was a possibility.

Mostly, they didn't want to go inside while Charley and George were in there, since they would most likely try to scare the girls, which would probably not work, especially after what they and Randolph had recently been through.

The boys went in and looked around for a while. At first, they were a little bit cowed by the flickering, electric torches and the generally scary atmosphere that couldn't seem to decide if malevolence or malfunction created the scene. They could see the girls walking back and forth outside the tent at odd intervals. On the last few passes the boys saw them eating hot dogs on a stick. The sight of hot dogs and their growing unease about the haunted house caused them to quickly look at each other and bolt for the food court.

On the way out, they started chanting, "scaredy-cats, scaredy-cats, the girls are scaredy-cats." This caused Miss Maya and Bits to glance at each other, nod their heads, and march into the haunted house with their heads held high and a resolute looks upon their faces. Randolph adopted a determined, but cautious, look as they entered the haunted house, which was actually a beat-up old tent. Miss Maya, Bits, and Randolph wandered around the various exhibits which seemed a bit passé. The "ghost" was a moldy looking old bed sheet with eyeholes cut in what passed for the face, which moved back and forth on what seemed to be a clothesline by a bored-to-stone teenager who was sitting on a rickety old folding chair directing his attention to his tablet more than anything else.

Just inside of the tent they ran across a threesome of rotten looking characters. The biggest was a man with large muscles and a fierce facial expression that seemed to be more or less permanent. It turned out that he was mute except for occasional grunts and growls. Second was a fat, disheveled, frumpy, unkept woman whose dress was ill-fitting and covered with multiple suspicious looking stains.

Her hair went in all sorts of directions, was of varying lengths, and had the general appearance of having been trimmed with a weed whacker. The third member of this disreputable looking trio was a wiry, dangerous looking man with a scraggly beard, beady eyes, and an unsheathed Bowie knife in his belt. They hung around the entrance trying to look fierce and dangerous which they had little trouble doing. The tacky trio made faces at the young man running the ropes of the "ghost" which he returned forthwith.

"These fakers have no idea what the supernatural is about, and even if they do know bits and pieces about the world of ghosts and spirits, they aren't taking much, if any, advantage of their knowledge," said Miss Maya. As they watched the manipulator of the sheet they noticed a faint, white mist forming behind him.

As the mist solidified into a roughly human shape, two arms materialized followed shortly by the rest of the apparition.

The first action of the phantasm was to push over the chair, dumping the teenager unceremoniously on the dirt floor of the tent. As he got up and dusted himself off, a deep voice seemed to come from everywhere and nowhere. Whereupon the manipulator of sheet ran out of there as if he was shot from a gun.

"Are you not frightened?" asked the voice.

"Well, your voice might scare some, but not us. We have seen way too much of the supernatural to have our knees knocking together just from a deep voice, although it does have a nice resonance," said Miss Maya.

"Speak for yourself Miss Maya. My knees are knocking together at a rapid rate that I don't much care for," said Randolph.

"You don't have knees Randolph, so get over it," said Bits.

"If I had knees they would be knocking together to beat the band," said Randolph giving Bits a dirty look.

"Do you girls, and of course Randolph, want to learn more of the ways of magic? I would be happy to teach you. I am so sick-to-death of the dullards who care only for passing tickles of pleasure when they pretend to be frightened which, given the shabby nature of the "ghost," is something they have to work hard to accomplish. The only thing I do is say a few words and the girls and women scream and run while boys and men just run, usually cussing a blue streak," said the voice.

"We would always like to know of new things, and knowledge in the field of magic is, as you know, quite valuable. Real magic is hard to come by and, depending on where it comes from, it can be either a great insight or total rubbish. Which of these do you have, Sir Voice?" asked Miss Maya. Bits and Randolph nodded their heads in agreement.

"Also, it seems like your voice isn't the same all of the time," said Bits.

"Actually, there are two of us here," said the deep, authoritative voice. "I am the first one that you heard. I have been a spirit for well over four thousand years. I have known the ways of magic ever since the ancient days of India, the Middle East, and beyond. The other voice is Arnold, he is a Union veteran of the Civil War and was killed at Antietam. He has been hanging around here for the last two hundred or so years. He can materialize and dematerialize any time he wants but he doesn't do it very often anymore since he appears to be so evil and fearsome that roughly half of the people who see him die on the spot from pure fear."

"Okay, trot out, poor old Arnold. Since the Civil War was a long time ago, even if he has several bullet holes in him, they should not be bleeding much by now. As we said before, we don't scare easily so go ahead and pop the cork on Arnold's bottle and let us have a look at him," said Bits.

Randolph, Bits, and Miss Maya looked around a bit and watched as Arnold slowly materialized. He wore a uniform that was full of holes. It was hard to decide if the uniform was blue or grey. The girls and Randolph stared at poor beat up old Arnold.

He didn't look particularly evil or fearsome. Scruffy and pathetic were much more accurate descriptions and closer to the mark than fearsome. It must have been quite some time since he had materialized since his image was faint and in spots could almost be seen through.

"I have a question for you, Arnold. How many people have actually fallen over dead from the fright they got by seeing you?" said Miss Maya. "I am thinking that if anyone died here at all it was from eating the corn dogs or tripping over the tent ropes."

"Well," said Arnold in a scratchy and not often used voice. "I am not good at numbers, and being a ghost and all, I can't remember much. So I would have to make a guess of about 10,000 or so, give or take 500."

"I would say that you should work on telling the truth before you go after the numbers," said Miss Maya.

During this exchange, Randolph had been watching Arnold carefully. He walked around Arnold looking up and muttering to himself. Finally, he said, "I have an extremely important question to ask you if you don't mind."

"Go ahead little bear," said Arnold.

"Are you going to gobble us up?" said Randolph.

"Randolph," said Bits in an indignant tone. "I don't think that a ghost can eat anything. Because if they could and since they are very faint you would be able to see what was in their stomachs."

"Oh, gross," said Randolph and Miss Maya at the same time.

"You don't have to worry about me gobbling you up since, as a ghost, I don't eat anything, but I sometimes suck energy out of living things to keep me from disappearing all together," said Arnold. "Do you children have any energy to spare? I could certainly use some. Human energy is the best and is the easiest. When I borrow energy from the circus lion or the elephant, they get quite annoyed and become so fierce that they go crazy and sometimes eat or trample the customers. So far, the Voice has looked out for me but he can't do it forever. If the manager knew it was me causing the animals to get spooky he would probably get an exorcist to put me in a jar and then throw me in the river."

"Ok, since the Voice is fronting for you, can you call him over so that we can get to know him?" asked Miss Maya.

"I can try," said Arnold. There followed a good deal of muttering, an occasional yell, some sort of whistling and finally, silence.

"I will meet with you," said the Voice as he slowly materialized. When he was fully visible, the apparition was very tall and muscular. He wore what looked like pajama bottoms and a vest with all sorts of designs and images on it. The longer that one looked at it, the more one could see tigers, snakes, and some sort of primitive hunters slowly coming forward. "Don't look at it for too long or it will pull you in and you will never get out," said the Voice.

"Can you please tell us your name?" said Miss Maya.

"Of course. It is, however, a bit complicated. My name is Azhuthavasan Bhoolokanathan. My first name means 'man of the river' and my last name means 'ruler over the earth.' Since humankind has made a mess of the world, I don't particularly want to be the ruler over the earth. The first name suits me best since I can see myself relaxing by a nice river, doing a bit of fishing and listening to the frogs. Since my names are long and complicated and since most Americans can't pronounce anything with more than a few syllables, you can use an abbreviation of my first name and call me 'Az,' which should suit us all just fine."

"Are you a wizard, Az?" asked Bits.

"Do you know any wizards?" replied Az.

"Yes, we do," said Miss Maya, Bits, and Randolph all at the same time.

"We know a magician named Marlin and have seen him do some pretty fantastic stuff, to the point of saving our lives on more than one occasion," replied Miss Maya. "Do you know him or have you heard of him?"

"Everyone in the field of magic and the occult knowledge knows of or has met the magician Myrddin Wyllt more commonly known as Merlin. But who is this Marlin that you speak of? I always thought that a Marlin was a fish," said Az.

"Well, yes, a marlin *is* a fish and the magician's name really is Merlin, but he changed it because he was sick-to-death of getting ads for time shares, insurance, investment schemes and such, so he changed his name to Marlin," said Miss Maya.

"We have been waiting for him to return, but he has been tied up trying to deal with a bunch of vampires. He should be arriving soon, hopefully without a bunch of holes in his neck," said Bits.

"Now I understand who Marlin is, but who are you?" asked Az.

"I'm Bits, short for Betsy. Next to me is Miss Maya and this scruffy little bear is Randolph."

"I would like to add 'Angelic Assistant Randolph.' I was given the title by the Angel Briathos," said a rather disgruntled Randolph.

"You all do indeed have a wide experience with the mysteries of the occult. I have run across Briathos a few times and have found him to be a good and decent being, but I never could figure out why he has all of those tattoos," said Az.

"I need to get Arnold back into the mystic realm where he won't need to use much, if any, energy to stay together. We will return when he is better," said Az.

As they started to move away from the entrance, the trashy trio began to take an interest in the children again. Seeing that there were two little girls and a beat-up old teddy bear they started to bully the children for money, food, etc. The three thugs became more and more aggressive. The girls and Randolph asked Az and Arnold to re-appear and they quickly did so.

They suggested that Arnold suck as much energy as he wants from the terrible trio and he did so post-haste.

CHAPTER 12

GOING HOME

When Arnold had gotten as much energy as he could hold, Az stepped forward and showed the thugs the stuff on his robes. They continued staring at Az's robe, got sucked in, and were heard from no more.

There soon followed a loud, earth-shaking thunder clap followed by a very strong wind, which stirred up a blinding amount of dust, leaves, twigs, branches, candy wrappers, soda cups, and a picnic basket. When the dust had settled, Marlin and Tamad emerged. Marlin looked somewhat the worse for wear even though his robe sparkled clean and all of the symbols on it looked brand new. Tamad seemed as frisky as a colt.

There was great shouting, hugging, giggling, and other antics while the children and Randolph pranced around in ecstasy. In the middle of all of the hubbub, Miss Maya's mom barreled into the tent looking for the children. Naomi almost passed out when she saw Marlin and Az. Seeing Arnold fading in and out didn't help matters much either.

"I can't believe my eyes. What is this? Who are these people? *Are* they people? What are you kids doing here?"

"It's okay, Mom," said Miss Maya. "We will explain everything. It may seem weird. It all fits together and makes sense of a sort, if you can re-think what you have believed all of these years."

"Okay Maya," said Naomi. "I will try to understand all of this, but as soon as we get home I will need a double Martini and to lie down with a cold cloth over my forehead for at least an hour."

"Thank you for being so understanding, Mom," said Miss Maya. "Bits and I have been familiar with the supernatural for quite a while. We are no longer afraid when we see it or experience it. No one has ever gotten hurt and we have learned a great deal. The only casualty is poor little Randolph getting the pants scared off of him, which is not easy since he doesn't wear pants. We would like you to ease into this, but if you want nothing to do with any of it we will understand. We know it is a lot to ask, but can Mr. Magician Marlin, Az, Tamad, and Arnold come home with us so everyone can be better acquainted?"

"Oh, my sweet Lord," said Naomi. "Okay, I guess it's fine. We can get Az, Arnold, and Mr. Magician Marlin in the car but not the horse.

"If I can be so bold as to suggest, perhaps I can ride on Tamad and follow the car," said Mr. Magician Marlin. "The young ladies and gentlemen, Randolph, Arnold, and Az can ride in the car. The house is only a few miles from here so the trip won't take long."

Miss Maya offered to sit next to her mother, but Naomi opted to have Az and Arnold sit in front with her, and have Bits, Miss Maya, and Randolph sit on the boys' laps which rounded out the arrangement. It seemed safer to have an ancient magician riding shotgun than fidgety little girls. They drove slowly so Marlin and Tamad could keep up. Fortunately, since Tamad had seen just about everything during his long life, there was little that would bother him. So, when a jerk in a white pickup came up behind them and started honking his horn, Tamad ignored him. However, the honking got on Marlin's nerves so he sent a lightning bolt calculated to hit just in front of the pickup. There was a huge racket, a large cloud of dust, and when it resolved the front wheels of the pickup were in the new hole in the road.

The driver of the pickup sat there staring blankly ahead looking like he had been hit over the head with a two-by-four piece of lumber. Naomi was startled, to say the least.

"The owner of that pickup is a guy named Robert who lives down the road from us," she said.

"Oh, I hope I didn't start a neighborhood feud," said Mr. Magician Marlin after pulling up parallel to the driver's side of the car.

"I would be delighted if you did. That guy is a total jerk so I would be deeply in your debt if you would turn him into a turnip or any other vegetable that resembles his IQ," said Naomi.

"I am very happy that you are not inconvenienced by my magic," said Mr. Magician Marlin. "I am not conversant with all of the ins and outs of the manner of speech of this time and place. Would I be too far off the mark if I suggested that "jerk" is similar to the appellation "knave" of my time?"

"You are spot on, Mr. Magician Marlin," said Naomi.

Things remained relatively quiet for the rest of the trip home except for the squirming and giggling of two very excited little girls. The boys tried to act cool but since the girls were sitting on their laps it was a bit hard to do. The only other sound was the snoring of Arnold and Az.

Charley told his sister to quit fidgeting so much. He received the reply that he should just shut up, Miss Maya's mom seconded the motion in the absence of Charley's mom, and, after that, silence reigned supreme. When they reached the house, Naomi suggested that she go in first to give her husband a heads-up. She didn't want to have this dropped on him all at once without any sort of warning. By the time everyone was out of the car or off of the donkey and into the house, things started to settle down.

Naomi and Ralph were introduced to everyone but they made their individual introductions on their own. It was a little easier for Naomi since she had a sort of running start. Ralph sat their looking dazed trying to figure out what was happening.

"Okay, I think I got it, "said Ralph. "Az is a wizard from the far east and has been around for a really long time. Marlin's real name is Merlin but he changed it so he wouldn't get bugged so much but it has nothing to do with fish. Marlin is a magician and has been one since the Middle Ages. Arnold was a casualty of the civil war and has a tough time getting by. I understand that there have been various adventures that involved demons, angels, large dangerous birds, fights between celestial beings, and all sorts of stuff. I have always been leery and cautious about anything that has to do with the supernatural. It has been like this since I was a small child. My father and his friend vanished many years ago and haven't been heard of since. Both of these girls are very intelligent and have very strong wills, but I don't think it is enough to allow them to grow up and get maimed, turned into a toad or vanished to some murky realm. I don't think that I can allow this to go forward. We will all break bread together and then you will all go your separate ways and these girls will go back to being children and growing into fine young women. I think it is good that they have had this exposure, but the risk is just too great. Does anyone have anything else to say? If not, it looks like the pizza just got here. I suggest that we don't let it get cold."

Things were somber with little talk while they all ate, some with more relish than others. The party dissolved quietly after dinner with most of the attendees fading away or simply vanishing. When all were gone except for the girls, Ralph called a meeting. They all sat around on various chairs, cushions, and the couch. There was a lot of staring at feet, fidgeting, and squirming. Ralph and Naomi sat side-by-side and looked at the floor.

"I am not at all well-versed or even minimally knowledgeable about this occult and supernatural stuff. All I know for sure is that this sort of thing took my father away from me and I never saw him again. I will not allow the same thing to happen to my daughter," said Ralph.

"Bits and I understand, Dad, but this sort of stuff isn't the kind of thing that can be turned on or off at will," said Miss Maya. "It is kind of like what I have heard you and Mom talk about when you are discussing the IRS. Once they get their hooks into you, it's hard to get them out. The supernatural and the magical realm are a little like that. Not too hard to get involved with but difficult to get rid of, which is not altogether bad. Depending on how things go on from here we might badly need the help of Mr. Magician Marlin, perhaps with reinforcements from Az if needed. He has proven himself to be very kind and caring. He came when we asked for his help and he generously gave it. I hope he is not upset with us."

CHAPTER 13

THE GATHERING STORM

Things were quiet for a few days after the pow-
wow and the pizza. At Naomi's direction Charley and George kept their distance from the
girls and pretty much left them alone except from
the occasional smart aleck remark. The role of being young gentlemen did not come easy to those two
rascals. They tried their best, or some approximation
of it, and to some degree were able to behave with

frowns and scowls from Miss Maya's mom. All concerned knew that the truce would not last forever.

During this time of trials the sky had become more and more cloudy. There wasn't much in the way of wind, no more than five knots at the worst. There was the same stillness that presages a thunderstorm with its silence and calm, but everyone was on edge waiting for the impending storm to come.

Things proceeded rapidly from this point forward, with the sky darkening to black with the wind picking up to 25 – 30 knots. A horrendous thunder clap caused the house to shake and sent poor Randolph diving head first under the coach. Charley and George would have followed Randolph, but they wouldn't fit under the couch, so they went into Charley's room and hid under the bed there instead.

"Hey, you scaredy-cat girls! Are you already shaking in your boots? Have you wet your pants yet? I'll bet you have. I wagered George dollars on it so it's time to pony up."

"Listen George and you too, Charley," said Miss Maya, "If you think about coming out here you better think again, because if you do get enough courage to get out from under the bed I will knock your teeth down your throat and spank you for swallowing them, so you had better think it over very carefully."

The girls understood their brothers to a "T" and stood just outside of the bedroom door. George and Charley very quietly slid out from under the bed. They were about 80% out from under it when Bits ducked into the room and tossed water on the front of George's pants.

"Well, look here, it looks like George had an accident in his pants. You are next Charley and make no mistake about it. Who's the scaredy-cat now among you tough guys? Wait until your homies at school find out about this. Too bad I don't have my camera. What a great picture for the school paper. I can already hear the laughter in the cafeteria."

After all of the referee and disciplinarian activities of the last few days, Miss Maya's mom was starting to spiral out of control. Her throat was sore from yelling at the young miscreants. She had just enough energy left to tell the girls not to throw water on Charley or any one else.

She made a last-ditch Kamikaze effort to obtain and maintain peace and calm. The results were heroic, but not very successful.

There was a hush in the wind, a quiet where nature seemed to be holding its breath. There followed a thunderous crashing noise as if the world had split in half. The first mega burst of thunder was followed by many more. Each one banging, shaking and following one after another. Some were so close together that it seemed like a horrendous attack was under way. The house shook, lamps broke, china spilled from the cupboards like an avalanche. Ralph ordered everyone into the basement and positioned them along the walls away from anything that might fall on them. George was allowed to go out of the basement for just long enough to call his parents on his cell phone to let them know that he was okay.

A short time after George returned to the basement and everything was buttoned down, everyone tried to relax, but to very little general effect. There was a pause in the noise of the storm, but no one was ready to believe that it was over. Instead of quiet for a time, the vacuum of the storm's noise was replaced by the sounds of footsteps of varying sizes on the floor above. They could hear bits and pieces of dialogue, but the language that was being used didn't sound very much like English. Someone, or several someones, began banging on the door at the top of the stairs and shouting for the occupants of the basement to come out. They had no intention of doing so but the choices seemed to be almost totally made by the attackers. Who they were and why there were making an attack was far from clear.

"Naomi," called Ralph. "Come here and help me get that old cabinet in the corner open and assist in distributing its contents."

The work was done in short order and each occupant of the basement was provided with a sword, spear, dagger, chain mail and a shield. These were handed out depending on the size of the recipient. Strangely enough there was even a size that fit Randolph to a "T." Randolph swaggered around for a time until the others reminded him that this was not a fashion show. The girls, after putting on their armor, were given the task of contacting Mr. Magician Marlin and Az. They were able to get in touch with them and the two sorcerers were to be there as quickly as they could.

"Dad, where did you get all of these weapons?" asked Miss Maya.

"Well, they are very old," said Ralph. "I used them a lot when I was in the Society for Creative Anachronisms. We had tournaments, jousting, and sword fights. You boys and the girls were in the junior division but still gave a good account of yourselves. We have to hold out until Marlin, Az, and Briathos can get here. Your mother and I will be in the front ranks. You two young ladies will be behind us. Randolph, you and the two boys attack from the second floor. You will have the high ground which is an advantage. You must do whatever you can to slow them down and do as much damage as possible, but don't give up the high ground under any circumstances. Keep your ranks tight and do not let the enemy get in between us.

"Remember that this is an old, fairly large house and because of its age there are two staircases from the basement to the first floor. Our enemies, who want to turn us into sausage, are currently on the first floor, rattling around to find a way to get down here and slice and dice us. I remember from my time in the military that the best defense is a good offense. By offense, I mean an attack and not the production of internal gas. Boys, go up the staircase to the second floor. When you hear me yell 'CHARGE' come running down the stairs from the second floor making all of the noise that you can. We will come roaring up the stairs from the basement and attack from that front.

We will, in effect, have them pinched between us. Will it be enough to carry the day? Maybe so. When and if our reinforcements get here we will let them take over. Any questions? Okay, let's go."

"Good heavens, Ralph," said Naomi. "You never saw five minutes of combat when you were in the army. Now you're acting like a general."

"Well, maybe not a shooting situation," replied Ralph. "However, maneuvering in the chow line was an art of no small sophistication, so please give me some credit."

The basement group gathered at the top of the stairs. Ralph yelled "CHARGE!" flung open the door and attacked. The group on the second floor ran down the stairs yelling like Banshees. Randolph made it about half way down the stairs before he realized that he was about to be trampled by his fellow soldiers. He gave as loud a yell as he was capable of and jumped off of the stairs, landing solidly a straddle the neck of one of the enemies, a great bruiser of a fellow, and proceeded to bang him on the head with the hilt of his sword. At first, other than bellowing and hollering, not much happened. However, the eyes of Randolph's opponent started to glaze over. Suddenly the galoot caved in and hit the floor. Charley reached down and snatched Randolph in the nick of time, keeping the giant from squashing poor Randolph flat. Both the basement and the second-floor teams were having an effect, but it seemed like the bad guys were being replaced as fast as they were dispatched. At first, the home team held its own, but the battle was slowly going in favor of the demons.

"We can't keep this up for much longer," said Ralph. "All of you keep your back to the wall so that no one can get behind you."

One of the demons threw a lightning bolt at Ralph. He jumped out of the way, but it grazed him on the side of the head knocking him to the floor.

"Dad!" yelled Miss Maya as she ran towards him.

"Leave me," said Ralph. "Keep fighting, it is our only chance." Things were getting worse by the minute.

There came a huge roaring noise and Marlin, Az, Briathos, and several other angels arrived in a tremendous flash of light. At first, everyone was blinded by it, but it resolved quickly enough. Glaysa Labolis found himself facing Briathos. Their last encounter had not turned out well for Glaysa Labolis and this one didn't look like it was going to be much better.

"I know that Gusion sent you," said Briathos. "If you don't want to get the same treatment as before, you had better make yourself scarce and do so quickly." Glaysa Labolis vanished at once in a puff of smoke along with some of the other demons who, all of a sudden, thought of places where they would rather be. With the departure of Glaysa Labolis and the appearance of Az and Marlin the battle was essentially over. The demonic combatants who had not worked on an escape route simply vanished. The defenders re-grouped and assessed their wounds which, thankfully, were not too bad. Marlin proceeded to treat them with various unguents and potions that eased the pain and caused rapid healing.

Az and Marlin huddled with Ralph and Naomi concerning the status of their house and what could be done to:

1) keep it from falling down and squashing someone or several someones

2) return it to its former glory, which was at its peak somewhere in the late 19th century and

3) making modernizing changes so the house would be more comfortable to live in. This last was championed by both Miss Maya and Charley, one of the few times that they agreed on anything. They could see glowing computer screens, a large panel TV, a huge swimming pool (Charley wanted it to be big enough for a submarine pen but had to settle for a diving board). Ralph had some bearer bonds that he would be able to cash in to get the necessary funds to bring about the changes that everyone wanted.

Things had wound down nicely when the doorbell rang and someone began banging on the door for all he was worth. When Ralph opened the door he saw a chunky man dressed in a cheap business suit carrying a battered brief case.

"My name is John Smith. I work for the Environmental Protection Agency. I am here to investigate a report of loud noises, smoke, fire, and a good deal of commotion. I need a full explanation of what has been going on here and I need to inspect the house to see if it can be inhabited. If it can't be brought back to normal, it will be condemned and you will have to relocate. Furthermore, I am informing you that the government will not pay for any relocation or repairs. You will be expected to reimburse us for any permits, plan inspection, and oversight. Do you understand this?"

Ralph looked at the pathetic specimen on his porch and shook his head in disbelief. "Is this what I pay the exorbitant taxes for that you guys charge? I am not much up on this sort of thing. However, I have a close friend who is, among other things, an expert in demolition and construction. We have the good fortune that he is visiting us today. He can represent us and answer your questions. He looks a little bit intimidating, but he is a good guy. It won't do, however, for you to try to bully him.

"Briathos, could you come out here and speak with this government official please?"

Briathos presented himself quickly and stood towering over Mr. Smith by several feet. "How may I be of service?" Briathos asked looking down on Mr. Smith. "My friends have been through a very tough time and I would not like to see them bullied by some government hack. They are good law-abiding citizens and I would be most unhappy if they were to be harassed and I am never unhappy alone. Do we understand each other?"

Smith's demeanor had gone from haughty to cowardice to sheer terror in the brief period of their conversation.

"Well, ah, well I guess that this is taken care of so I will just be moving along. Good day to you folks," said the stalwart government official as he made a break for his old rattle trap of a government car. His hands shook so badly that he dropped his car keys five times before he got the car door open. Once inside the car he started the engine and proceeded to floor it, causing a noxious blast of exhaust that, due to the car's advanced age, looked like ten miles of bad road. Briathos put his foot on the rear bumper and gave it a shove of such intensity that black marks were left on the road as the car careened out of sight. It was later learned that Mr. Smith left government service and became an insurance salesman.

When it was at last over, Ralph thanked Briathos, letting him know how very grateful they all were for the help that they had received.

"You are most welcome," said Briathos. "I will let Mr. Magician Marlin and Az deal with the rest of this. The young ladies know how to reach me if you require my services," with that and the customary large puff of smoke, Briathos disappeared.

CHAPTER 14

WRAP UP

I t didn't take much time before things got back to "normal" with Mis Maya, Bits, and Randolph. There were games of croquet and various other games that they made up as they went along. It didn't take long for the girls and Randolph to get a bit bored. The new swimming pool kept George and Charley occupied for the rest of the summer, but the girls got tired of wet swimming suits and their maintenance.

"I'm bored, even the swimming pool is getting a little tiresome," said Bits. "Nothing is happening here. I think we are going to be throwing dirt up in the air soon if nothing interesting happens."

"Bits," said Miss Maya, "Remember how this all started? I think we have had enough excitement for a while."

"I think that you are right, mayonnaise. Let's just wait until school starts. Maybe there will be some cute boys for us to get to know," said Bits.

As it turned out, there were several to choose from.

The girls and Randolph wandered down by the bridge where so much of their adventure took place. It looked like the simple, old bridge that it was, no reminders of all that had happened here. The breeze shifted the branches, dropping leaves onto the quiet scene below.

Suddenly, Marlin and Tamad appeared, crossing the bridge toward them. It had been awhile and the sight of their faces inspired quite the delight. The girls and Randolph jumped up and down, waving at Marlin. Marlin returned the favor by shouting, "We are not done with this yet. I think that there is much more to come!"

And with that, both Marlin and Tamad vanished in a puff of smoke.

ABOUT THE AUTHOR

Norman Baron is an avid, voracious, and broad-based reader. Now, at last, he has the time to write full-time. He has written a book for and about his granddaughter, who is a delight to be around. Her name is Maya. She inspired him to write this book because of her wit, smartness, and rascally personality.

Norman loves to fly. He has been a pilot of single and multi-engine planes for years, and at one time, owned a hot air balloon. Norman was a vascular and general surgeon in a rural underserved area in the desert of Southern California, near the Mexican border, for over 40 years.

After retirement, he moved to Arizona with his wife to spend more time with their granddaughter, Maya.

Made in the USA
Middletown, DE
27 September 2021